For the children of the sun and the sky that keeps us

Thank you Molly for the intricate wonder of your mind.
The universe we've created is a dream come true.

- A.L.

For Ayoola and Lilly

Thank you to Amyra for allowing me
to bring images to your voice.

- M.M.

Freedom, We Sing © Flying Eye Books 2020.

First edition published in 2020 by Flying Eye Books, an imprint
of Nobrow Ltd. 27 Westgate Street, London, E8 3RL.

Text © Amyra León 2020
Illustrations © Molly Mendoza 2020

1 3 5 7 9 10 8 6 4 2

Published in the US by Nobrow (US) Inc.
Printed in Latvia on FSC® certified paper.

ISBN: 978-1-912497-32-4
www.flyingeyebooks.com

AMYRA LEÓN · MOLLY MENDOZA

FREEDOM, WE SING

FLYING EYE BOOKS
LONDON | NEW YORK

Families of stars
Surround me
Every constellation
Humming a different
Melody

Sometimes the world

Seems so small

I pretend to put it in my palm

I dance with her
Till night falls
And the moon
Comes swaying in

Giving the sun
Time to rise
On all the other kin

Inhale.

Exhale.

Mama tells me that
There are children
With hearts like mine
Beat beat beating
In their chests

With different skin colors
Hair, languages, and interests
They learn to walk and talk
And dance and scream

Just like me
Or anybody

Inhale.

Exhale.

Mama tells me that
There are mothers
With hearts like ours
Beat beat beating
In their chests

Running from war
With whatever is left
Doing everything
They can to protect
Their children
And their breath

Inhale.

Exhale.

I wonder then
What Freedom is

Is it a place?
Is it a thought?
Can it be stolen?
Can it be bought?

Does Freedom run through our veins?
Can it be equal and maintained?

Do I have it?
Do I not?
Can it be written?
Can it be taught?

Inhale.

Exhale.

Mama tells me
Breath is Freedom
A sweet release
The right to be

A universal sign
Of life and peace

The sky is our equality
It unites us with the world
And our ancestry

Inhale.

Breath is what makes us alive
It is a chance to swallow the sky

Breath is a reminder that
History is everywhere

We are the answer
To our ancestors' prayers

May we dance into the sunrise

May we believe in our dreams

May we learn the song of Freedom
That the constellations sing

Inhale.

Freedom is you
Freedom is me